The Incredible Indian REVOLUTIONARIES QUIZ

Chiranjit Gam is an educator for Civil Services Examination preparation in several institutes in Guwahati, Assam. He has been engaged in teaching and training programmes in the capacity of visiting resource person at Pre-Examination Training Centre—Gauhati University and Assam Administrative Staff College. He has also been serving as teaching faculty for the coaching programme under State Level Advisory Committee, Government of Assam, for the last couple of years.

Chiranjit is a renowned quizmaster from Assam, having conducted several live quiz competitions across the country. A few notable ones are at Indian Institute of Technology, Kharagpur; IIT-BHU, Varanasi; National Institute of Technology, Allahabad; and Tezpur University.

He can be reached at chiranjit.gam@gmail.com

The Incredible Indian REVOLUTIONARIES QUIZ

CHIRANJIT GAM

RUPA

Published by
Rupa Publications India Pvt. Ltd 2019
7/16, Ansari Road, Daryaganj
New Delhi 110002

Sales centres:
Allahabad Bengaluru Chennai
Hyderabad Jaipur Kathmandu
Kolkata Mumbai

ISBN: 978-93-5333-720-9

First impression 2019

10 9 8 7 6 5 4 3 2 1

Printed at HT Media Ltd, Gr. Noida

In loving memory of my father, Bimal Gam,
who sowed the seeds of curiosity in me.

This book is dedicated to the sacrifices made by the names close to our hearts, names lesser known and countless others unknown. These noble souls not only fought for our Independence but also secured the destiny of the future generations—something we all should be eternally thankful for.

CONTENTS

Foreword ix

Introduction xi

1. Know Your Heroes 1
2. History, as It Unfolds 7
3. Facts of the Past 12
4. The Known and the Unknown 18
5. Facets of the Indian Freedom Struggle 24
6. Historical Potpourri 31
7. Sacrifices Galore 39
8. Books and Authors 47
9. Newspapers, Journals and Magazines 50
10. Early Political Associations 53
11. Revolutionary History–I 56
12. Notes, Quotes and Anecdotes 63
13. The Press 67
14. Policies on Education 71
15. Revolutionary History–II 75
16. Take It Easy 83

Author's Note 89

Acknowledgements 90

FOREWORD

Many centuries ago, the world started to evolve as humans formed groups called *tribes*. The world today has perhaps come full circle with just a simple prefix being added. Now we are all part of a *knowledge tribe,* which some call the knowledge economy. Some say knowledge is the new oil; some call it the currency of the future. The need for knowledge is so high that on any given day, we seek and share knowledge using every conceivable medium possible. The sheer quantum of information being produced and consumed in the world is incredible.

This explosion of information has not only opened up industry and is shaping a future society in real time, but it has also led to a huge growth in quizzing across the world, including in India. Every school, college, university and company today hosts its share of quizzes, and the knowledge sport has become an integral part of learning. Technology has brought quizzing into our hands, with apps aplenty quizzing us on our understanding of the world.

Our Mahatma once said, 'Live as if you were to die tomorrow. Learn as if you were to live forever.' It is so true in the current world we live in. Having a broader knowledge of the world makes us better communicators. Some of the core future skills that will enable success include knowledge and communication, both of which are enabled by quizzing.

As a quizmaster, I have often wondered if I am a seeker, a sharer, or both. Despite being perceived as a sharer, numerically if I were to map it, the learner in me (seeker) outdoes the sharer. In simple terms, what I learn or seek (that is new) is far more than what I share (what I had learnt earlier). Quizzers by default are from the Seeker Tribe. It is wonderful to see youngsters like Chiranjit sharing their repository with us. Knowledge is of no use unless you are willing to share it.

What I also appreciate is the choice of subject. Indian revolutionaries, A.P.J. Abdul Kalam and Swami Vivekananda, and Indian scientists are arguably far more relevant in the modern era than ever before, as youngsters seem to know more of the world than our own country and countrymen.

While I wish Chiranjit the very best with this series and more to come, I wish more youngsters are inspired to write books that feature their research.

May the tribe grow!

Giri Balasubramaniam

Popularly known as 'Pickbrain', he is a noted quizmaster and a TED speaker, who has presented more than 2,000 shows across nine countries. His company, Greycaps, has pioneered classroom-based programmes in general knowledge and value education, with schools across Asia catering to over 16 million youngsters. He has a master's in Media Management, a master's in Gandhian Philosophy and is an alumnus of the prestigious Harvard Business School in Boston, Massachusetts.

INTRODUCTION

The first and simplest emotion which we discover in the human mind is curiosity.

—Edmund Burke,
Anglo-Irish statesman and philosopher

Quizzing, contrary to popular notion, does not merely deal with gulping down bookish information or parroting events. Rather, it is a continuous activity of seeking answers to even trivial facts, which stems from sheer curiosity. Quizzing deals with anything and everything under the sun, from Gandhi to Gandalf, George Best to George Bush, Kubrick to Kilpatrick, and Tata to Toyota. Literally everything. As such, the flow of information can never be directed to a singular origin.

There are no prescribed directives to becoming a good quizzer. However, a curious mind and an observant self go a long way in proving one's mettle. Quizzing, just like evolution, is a continuous process. One can learn a lot from what one sees or hears in one's daily life. The joy of knowing a fact hidden in plain sight is sublime and inexplicable. I still recall the day I came to know that the

BSA in BSA Cycles stood for Birmingham Small Arms, a company whose primary products were not cycles but artillery guns. I owned a BSA cycle in sixth standard. Of course, I did not know the fact then, but when I did, it was such a wonderful feeling!

During the pre-Internet days, one had to resort to books, newspapers and journals. I recall, while I was in school, my father would buy me a magazine called *Wisdom* every fortnight. *Wisdom* was priced at ₹5 then. That was probably the time I imbibed the habit of collecting and knowing information. I would re-read the facts in *Encyclopedia Britannica* in my spare time at the school library and keep cutouts, maintain a diary and constantly look for unusual facts in newspapers.

With the advent of the Internet and smartphones, information has become easily accessible. One can follow myriad quizzing websites, forums and pages to get a sense of the sheer volume of knowledge floating around.

For many, including me, who have devoted a fair amount of time in the name of quizzing, it is an emotion. The butterflies in your stomach you feel a day before a good quiz, the rush of blood when you answer a question correctly, working out an answer from the question when you do not know the answer. Ah! Pure joy!

From winning school- and college-level quizzes to open quizzes and finally to becoming a quizmaster, I have seen and experienced it all. It is an activity everybody should participate in and encourage others to, too.

For budding quizzers, I would highly advise reading more. Nothing beats reading a good book. Reading helps nurture curious young minds. Retention is key. Cultivate the habit of participation and competition. You might not win a quiz competition right away, but eventually, you definitely will. Quizzing is an activity or a hobby that keeps the grey cells sharp and active. It is an exercise of the brain.

I recall the late legendary quizmaster Neil O'Brien, who once said, 'There are questions, the answer of which no one knows, there are questions, the answer of which everyone knows, but there will be questions, which only you will know. And then you will realize how different you are from the rest.'

1

KNOW YOUR HEROES

1. Hussainiwala, a sleepy remote village located in present-day Pakistan, was officially taken back by the Indian government on 17 January 1961 from Pakistan in exchange for 12 Indian villages. Why is the place Hussainiwala of such importance to India?
2. Fondly known as 'Master Da' because he was a schoolteacher, this famous Indian revolutionary was the head of the Chittagong Raid on the police armoury in 1930. The 2010 Bollywood movie *Khelein Hum Jee Jaan Sey* was based on his life and his revolutionary activities. Who am I taking about?
3. The Pravasi Bharatiya Divas, or the Overseas Indian Day, is celebrated on 9 January every year in India. Why was the specific day chosen to celebrate this?
4. Formerly known as the Pacific Coast Hindustan Association, this famous Indian revolutionary organization was founded in 1913 with its headquarters in San Francisco. Interestingly, etymologically, the name of the organization in Urdu means 'Revolt'. Lala

Har Dayal, Kartar Singh Sarabha and Sohan Singh Bhakna were a few of the popular founding members of the organization. What was the organization known as?

5. Conceived by Ram Prasad Bismil and Ashfaqulla Khan, the Kakori Train Robbery, which took place in present-day Uttar Pradesh on 9 August 1925, is one of the most defining and valiant incidents in the history of India. Which Indian revolutionary organization was responsible for the Kakori Train Robbery?
6. She was one of the most prominent figures in the Indian Independence movement. In 1896, she volunteered to help the victims of the bubonic plague that broke out in the Bombay presidency. However, she contracted the plague herself. Owing to her poor health, she had to leave for London for medical care, where she spent most of her life. Later, on 22 August 1907, she became the first Indian to hoist the Indian flag on foreign soil, in Stuttgart, Germany. Who was she?
7. Almost immediately after Mahatma Gandhi launched the Salt Satyagraha from Dandi in 1930, several other movements to break salt laws erupted in several parts of the country. One of the most significant was in Tamil Nadu. Who led the salt march in Tamil Nadu?
8. Which eminent educationist became the defending lawyer for the group of accused revolting Indians that attacked the police station in Chauri Chaura, Gorakhpur, in 1922? The event eventually led to the withdrawal of the Non-Cooperation Movement in India by Mahatma Gandhi. It is noteworthy that this personality was also

posthumously conferred the Bharat Ratna in 2014 for his stellar contribution to Indian Independence and the Indian education system.

9. She is widely remembered for hoisting the Indian National Congress flag at the Gowalia Tank in Bombay (now Mumbai) during the Quit India Movement in 1942. An active member of the Indian freedom movement, she earned the titles of 'Heroine of 1947' and 'The Grand Old Lady of Independence' due to her bravery and courage. Who was she?

10. Which famous slogan was coined by the Urdu poet and Indian freedom fighter Maulana Hasrat Mohani in 1929 that became the rally cry of the Indian Independence movement?

11. According to historians worldwide, a French revolutionary named Auguste Vaillant hurled a bomb in the French parliament in 1893 to protest against oppressive French policies. This inspired a famous incident during the Indian freedom struggle. What was the incident?

12. In 1893, Lokmanya Bal Gangadhar Tilak revived an event to make the bond between the upper and the lower castes of society stronger, as well as to bring about a strong sense of unity and nationalism among Indians. This was done so that Indians could come together to collaboratively fight against British rule in India. What did Tilak do?

13. Acclaimed writer-activist Mahasweta Devi's award-winning novel *Aranyer Adhikar* is based on the life of which tribal freedom fighter known for his strong revolt

against British rule and its anti-tribal agrarian policies?

14. She was born on 26 January 1915 in Manipur. At the young age of 13, she joined the Heraka movement, a Naga religious movement that later turned into a political one to drive out the British from Manipur and the surrounding Naga areas. Known as a master tactician in guerrilla warfare, she was given the title of 'Rani' (queen) by Jawaharlal Nehru for her bravery. Identify the legendary freedom fighter.

15. He was referred to as the 'Manyam Veerudu' (Hero of the Jungles) by the locals of Andhra Pradesh. He led the famous Rampa Rebellion in 1922–24 against British rule in the Madras presidency. Identify the famous revolutionary after whom the cricket stadium in Eluru is named.

16. Which dreadful event in Indian history occurred when people gathered to protest against the arrest of two prominent freedom fighters of Punjab, Dr Saifuddin Kitchlew and Dr Satyapal, on 9 April 1919?

17. Along with Mohan Singh and Pritam Singh Dhillon, which unsung Indian revolutionary and freedom fighter is credited with organizing and founding the Indian National Army?

18. To achieve an independent, united and secular India, which non-Indian Bharat Ratna award winner had started an organization called the Khudai Khidmatgar (Servants of God), also known as the 'Red Shirt Army', to end British rule in India?

19. An ardent follower of Mahatma Gandhi, this prominent revolutionary and freedom fighter from Assam is

considered the only martyr in India to have been hanged in the last phase of the Quit India Movement. He was accused of derailing a train that was carrying British soldiers in a place called Sarupathar. Name him.

20. Established by Pramathanath Mitra in 1902, this secret society played a significant role in revolutionary and radical activities during the Indian freedom struggle. Name this secret society, which was initially set up as a 'bodybuilding society'.

ANSWERS

1. Hussainiwala is the crematory ground of the revolutionaries Bhagat Singh, Shivaram Rajguru and Sukhdev Thapar.
2. Surya Sen.
3. The day marks Mahatma Gandhi's return to India from South Africa in 1915.
4. Ghadar Party.
5. Hindustan Socialist Republican Association (HSRA). It later came to be known as Hindustan Socialist Republican Army.
6. Bhikaji Cama.
7. C. Rajagopalachari.
8. Madan Mohan Malviya.
9. Aruna Asaf Ali.
10. *Inquilab Zindabad!* (Long Live the Revolution!)
11. Bhagat Singh and Batukeshwar Dutt hurled a bomb at the Central Legislative Assembly on 8 April 1929, a momentous incident in the Indian freedom struggle.

12. He popularized the large-scale celebration of Ganesh Chaturthi (Ganapati festival) in India.
13. Birsa Munda.
14. Rani Gaidinliu (aka Naga Rani Lakshmi Bai).
15. Alluri Sitarama Raju.
16. The Jallianwala Bagh tragedy in Amritsar.
17. Rash Behari Bose.
18. Khan Abdul Ghaffar Khan (aka Bacha Khan).
19. Kushal Konwar.
20. Anushilan Samiti.

DID YOU KNOW?

Rabindranath Tagore composed two songs to express his grief over the Partition of Bengal, which occurred in 1905. One was *Amar Sonar Bangla*, which later became the national anthem of Bangladesh, and the other was *Ekla Cholo Re*, a song of patriotism.

2

HISTORY, AS IT UNFOLDS

1. With help from Lala Lajpat Rai, which institution did Dayanand Saraswati establish to impart unbiased and nationalistic education to the youth of India during British rule?
2. Whom did Sri Aurobindo (also known as Aurobindo Ghose) refer to as one of the mightiest prophets of nationalism during the Indian freedom struggle, who is also known as 'the father of revolutionary thoughts'?
3. The Santhal Rebellion, a violent tribal movement, started in 1855 against the despotic taxation system of the British in present-day Jharkhand. Name the two revolutionaries who started the Santhal Rebellion, after whom a public university in Jharkhand is named?
4. A Parsee intellectual and social leader, he is best known for his revolutionary writings on the economic exploits of the British in India. His most famous work, *Poverty and Un-British Rule in India,* dealt with the economic-drain theory for the first time. He was instrumental in framing the Bombay Plan—the first attempt in India

to have a structured economic-planning process. Who was he?

5. Whose final resting place is in the compound of the Renkō-ji Temple in Tokyo, where the ashes are stored in a golden pagoda?
6. The founder of the Indian National Association and the Indian National Liberation Federation, he is remembered as a pioneer in Indian politics. He was the editor of a newspaper called *The Bengalee*. In 1883, he was arrested for publishing anti-British articles. He was elected as the president of the Indian National Congress in 1895 and again in 1902. Who was he?
7. She was an active revolutionary since her childhood days. She formed the organizations Mrityu Bahini and Shanti Bahini, pledging supreme sacrifice for India's Independence. She began Individual Satyagraha in Assam on the advice of Mahatma Gandhi. Name the braveheart, who later became a member of the Rajya Sabha from Assam.
8. Which lesser-known freedom fighter from Rajasthan, who played an active part in the Non-Cooperation Movement, wrote the revolutionary books named *Azadi Ke Diwane* and *Jaisalmer Ka Gundaraj*?
9. Which revolutionary and Indian freedom activist formed a revolutionary group called Ramoshi, to overthrow the British Raj in the Deccan region? Due to his contributions, efforts and tactics, he is also known as 'the father of armed rebellion in India'.
10. Known as the 'immortal warrior', which historical Khasi leader from Meghalaya led a battalion of soldiers

and used guerrilla tactics to fight the British troops in the Khasi hills, which eventually resulted in the Anglo-Khasi War of 1829?

11. These three prominent revolutionaries were keen followers of Bal Gangadhar Tilak, who formed a secret society named Binashi Samity in Pune to fight against British rule. They shot dead W.C. Rand, the plague commissioner in 1896, due to his oppression and brutality towards plague-affected people in Pune. Identify them.

12. Popularly known as 'Old Lady Gandhi', she was a fierce revolutionary who was shot dead in front of the Tamluk police station by British soldiers for participating in revolutionary activities. During the Quit India Movement, she famously led a group of 6,000 volunteers, most of them women. At the time of her death, she firmly held the Indian National Congress flag and repeated the words '*Vande Mataram*'. Who is she?

13. The much popular Hindu devotional song 'Raghupati Raghava Raja Ram' (aka Ram-dhun) was widely popularized by Mahatma Gandhi during the Dandi March. Who originally put the lyrics to the music?

14. Due to which incident in 1922 did Mahatma Gandhi call off the Non-Cooperation Movement, as he said it opposed the ideologies of non-violence?

15. During his teenage years, he set up a youth organization called Mitra Mela (Band of Friends) to embrace revolutionary and nationalist ideas. Identify the revolutionist who later received a 50-year jail term for plotting an armed rebellion against the Morley-Minto

Reforms in 1909.

16. In 1930, what did Dr Kanuga famously and successfully bid for $750, then worth ₹1,600?
17. Henry David Thoreau, who championed the ideology of the free spirit, was an American author, poet and philosopher. Which ideology of Thoreau is said to have inspired Mahatma Gandhi, which he later implemented during the Indian freedom movement?
18. A qualified educationist, he was the first Indian to pursue an Economics doctorate abroad. His famous book, *The Problem of the Rupee: Its Origin and Its Solution,* laid the guidelines for the establishment of the Reserve Bank of India in 1923. However, he is best known for his crusade for minority rights and the establishment of the Indian Constitution. Identify him.
19. Which popular patriotic song written by Bismil Azimabadi was immortalized by the revolutionary Ram Prasad Bismil as a freedom war cry against the British Raj in India?
20. A contemporary of Mahatma Gandhi, what is freedom fighter Pingali Venkayya's most remembered contribution to the country?

ANSWERS

1. Dayanand Anglo Vedic (D.A.V.) schools and institutions.
2. Bipin Chandra Pal.
3. Sidhu Murmu and Kanhu Murmu. The university is the Sido Kanhu Murmu University.

4. Dadabhai Naoroji.
5. Subhas Chandra Bose.
6. Sir Surendranath Banerjee.
7. Pushpalata Das.
8. Sagarmal Gopa.
9. Vasudev Balwant Phadke.
10. U Tirot Sing Syiem.
11. The Chapekar brothers—Damodar Hari Chapekar, Balkrishna Hari Chapekar and Vasudeo Hari Chapekar.
12. Matangini Hazra.
13. Vishnu Digambar Paluskar.
14. The Chauri Chaura incident.
15. Vinayak Damodar (V.D.) Savarkar, along with the contributions of his brother Ganesh Savarkar.
16. The first lump of salt held by Mahatma Gandhi during the Dandi March.
17. Civil disobedience or passive resistance.
18. Dr Bhim Rao (B.R.) Ambedkar.
19. 'Sarfaroshi Ki Tamanna'.
20. He designed the Indian national flag

DID YOU KNOW?

Audi has restored the historic German Wanderer sedan, in which Subhas Chandra Bose fled house arrest by British officials in 1941. The Netaji Research Bureau currently maintains the car. It bears the original registration number BLA 7169.

3

FACTS OF THE PAST

1. This 'instrument' was both a tool and a symbol during India's freedom movement. The two most popular variants of this 'instrument' are the bardoli and the peti. Which instrument is it?
2. Independence Day in Mauritius is celebrated every year on 12 March—a date that is special to all Indians. Which prominent event took place on this day in 1930?
3. Under the Tinkathia system, the British forced the native peasants of Champaran (Bihar) to cultivate 3 kathaa of indigo in every 20 kathaa (1 bigha) of land. To abolish this illegal method of cultivation, what did the peasants, along with Mahatma Gandhi and Rajendra Prasad, start in the early part of the nineteenth century?
4. Potti Sreeramulu was a renowned Indian revolutionary during the British India era. After Independence, he died due to a 58-day hunger strike against the Government of India. After his death, his demand was

eventually accepted by the government. What was his demand and what did it lead to the creation of?

5. Which freedom fighter authored *Gita Rahasya*, a vivid commentary on and translation of the Bhagavad Gita into Marathi, during his days of imprisonment in Mandalay, Myanmar?

6. He is known as 'the Otto von Bismarck of India', for integrating all the princely states into India after Independence. We celebrate his birthday as the Rashtriya Ekta Diwas, or National Unity Day. Who is he?

7. He is known as 'the father of Indian ornithology' due to his notable research on the study of birds in India. However, he is best known in Indian history for his pivotal role in setting up the Indian National Congress in 1885. Who am I talking about?

8. The Bengali novel *Anandamath* by Bankim Chandra Chattopadhyay was set in the backdrop of the devastating Bengal famine of 1770 and the Sannyasi rebellion against the British East India Company of the late eighteenth century. The novel was later banned by the British for awakening nationalist fervour amongst Indians against the British government. What is the most important contribution of the novel to India's freedom struggle?

9. At a very young age, this famous personality formed an army of child volunteers called 'Vanar Sena' (monkey brigade), through which she encouraged them to take part in the freedom struggle against the British. As many as 60,000 young revolutionaries became part of

the cause. Identify the personality, who later went on to make a mark of her own in Indian politics.

10. Often known as 'the father of economic reforms in India', he brought a revolutionary change in the Indian economic sector by dismantling the Licence Raj and ushering in liberalization and globalization in the country. His critically acclaimed novel, *The Insider,* is a vivid account of his life and political career. Who is he?

11. Years before the world knew of Rani Laxmi Bai of Jhansi, this brave queen from South India was known as the 'first queen to fight against the British'. A valorous queen, she was a master of tactical warfare and intelligence-gathering. The Tamil people lovingly call her 'Veeramangai', meaning 'brave woman'. Identify her.

12. A patron of non-violence, social equality and human rights, this freedom activist is best known for starting the Bhoodan Movement in India, wherein landless people were given land from wealthy landowners. Mahatma Gandhi chose him as the first Individual Satyagrahi in 1940. In 1958, he was the first recipient of the international Ramon Magsaysay Award for community leadership. Identify this famous personality.

13. With the aim of giving marginalized people a dignified life through self-reliance and restoration of the sense of belonging that they had lost due to ill treatment at the hands of society, this revolutionary set up Anandwan in 1949 to provide services in the field of healthcare, education, agriculture and agro-industries, and small-

and medium-scale industrial units. In his days during the Indian freedom struggle, he had launched a vigorous protest against the British for disrespecting Indian women, which led Mahatma Gandhi to give him the title 'Abhay Sadhak' (fearless seeker of truth). Who am I referring to?

14. Regarded as one of the pillars of the Bengal renaissance, poet Michael Madhusudan Dutta referred to this person as having 'the genius and wisdom of an ancient sage, the energy of an Englishman and the heart of a Bengali mother'. A celebrated social activist who extensively worked for women's empowerment, his book, *Borno Porichoy*, is used as the introductory text to learning the Bengali alphabet. Who was he?

15. This prominent social reformer and thinker from nineteenth-century Maharashtra formed the Satya Shodhak Samaj to fight caste rigidity, Brahmin supremacy and the evil social practices prevalent in the country. Identify this social reformer, who is also widely considered the first Hindu to have established an orphanage in the country.

16. What was the apt name of the famous play by Dinabandhu Mitra which was about the Indigo Revolt of 1859 in Bengal, when farmers refused to sow indigo in their fields as a means of protest against the British agrarian and taxation policies?

17. 'The Philosophy of Bomb' is a famous document by an Indian revolutionary that was written as a rebuttal to Mahatma Gandhi's article 'The Cult of the Bomb', in which the latter had criticized revolutionary activities

in India. Identify the revolutionary who was strongly associated with the activities of the Hindustan Socialist Republican Association, along with Bhagat Singh, Sukhdev and Chandra Shekhar Azad.

18. A socioeconomic revolutionist, he is a Bharat Ratna and Ramon Magsaysay awardee for his significant contributions to the fields of social work and public service. Identify the famous personality who is known to have drafted the Sarvodaya Plan in 1950 and authored the book on economy *Why Socialism?*.
19. Known as the 'first nationalist English poet of modern India', he started the Young Bengal Movement to rally the youth of India for the national cause and for social awakening. Who is he?
20. A prominent social reformer and educationist, Gopal Ganesh Agarkar was one of the first individuals to have advocated the power of human reason. He was also the first editor of *Kesari*, a weekly newspaper founded by Lokmanya Tilak. Which important society did Gopal Ganesh Agarkar co-establish for the uplift of the socio-educational scenario in Maharashtra?

ANSWERS

1. The charkha (spinning wheel).
2. The Dandi March.
3. The Champaran Satyagraha.
4. Andhra Pradesh, India's first linguistic state.
5. Bal Gangadhar Tilak.
6. Sardar Vallabhbhai Patel.

7. Allan Octavian Hume.
8. The Indian national song, 'Vande Mataram', was first published in this novel.
9. Indira Gandhi.
10. P.V. Narasimha Rao.
11. Rani Velu Nachiyar.
12. Acharya Vinoba Bhave.
13. Baba Amte.
14. Ishwar Chandra Vidyasagar.
15. Jyotirao Phule.
16. *Nil Darpan* (The Indigo Planting Mirror).
17. Bhagwati Charan Vohra.
18. Jayaprakash Narayan.
19. Henry Louis Vivian Derozio.
20. Deccan Education Society.

DID YOU KNOW?

In 1835, the British government formed a paramilitary force called the Cachar Levy, a police unit for the protection of the English settlements against tribal attacks and other assaults during British occupation in Northeast India. It was renamed multiple times, and it gradually evolved to become India's oldest paramilitary force, The Assam Rifles.

4

THE KNOWN AND THE UNKNOWN

1. Which revolutionary movement was started by Periyar E.V. Ramasamy in the south to fight against Brahmin supremacy and dominion over caste, society, politics and religion in India and to bring about social change and equality among the various castes of India?
2. Which historical event did Lord Irwin call a 'storm in a tea cup', saying that Mahatma Gandhi's movement against them was at a 'kindergarten stage' of revolution?
3. Who was the only Indian to have participated in all the three Round Table Conferences with the British government?
4. Mahatma Gandhi once commented on a British attempt that it was 'a post-dated cheque on a crashing bank', rejecting the British offer of granting India dominion status and setting up an interim Indian government if Indians aided the British during the Second World War. What was this failed attempt by the British?
5. If Lal Bahadur Shastri coined the slogan '*Jai Jawan, Jai Kisan*' during the Indo-Pak War of 1965, who is

credited with the coining of the slogan '*Jai Jawan, Jai Kisan, Jai Vigyan*'?

6. Which Indian poet and lyricist wrote '*Vishwa Vijay Tiranga Pyara, Jhanda Ooncha Rahe Hamara*', which is accepted as the official national flag song of India? Interestingly, the song also featured in the 1948 film *Azadi Ki Raah Par*, sung by Sarojini Naidu.
7. First published in *Tattwabodhini Patrika*, the journal of the non-disintegrated Brahmo Samaj, what is also known as the 'Morning Song of India'?
8. *Bharat Ek Khoj* is a 53-episode Indian historical television drama that deals with the philosophy of Indian life during the ancient, medieval and modern eras. This series was directed, written and produced by Shyam Benegal. On which book was the TV series based?
9. Which famous Indian social reformer published the book *The Precepts of Jesus*, in which he depicted Jesus as a great teacher of ethics and harmony, and appealed for national integration?
10. Which movement, by Bhagat Jawahar Mal, was started as a religious movement to reform the Sikh religion in 1872, but eventually changed course and became a political struggle against British rule in India?
11. This historical task took 2 years, 11 months and 17 days to complete. Its original final form was handwritten by Prem Behari Narain Raizada in his own impeccable recognizable calligraphy. What was the outcome of this task?

12. The Aravipuram Movement by Sri Narayana Guru and the Vaikom Satyagraha by K.P. Kesava in Kerala had set the foundation of which nationwide movement in India for socio-religious equality?
13. Which prominent Indian Independence activist is credited with being the first to call the Revolt of 1857 'the First War of Independence'?
14. Since time immemorial, the Ottoman caliph is regarded as the supreme religious and political leader of all Sunni Muslims around the world. However, during the First World War, the Ottoman Empire suffered defeat at the hands of the Axis powers. The empire fell and its territorial boundaries were significantly reduced. Deeply upset by these events, which mass movement against the British did Maulana Mohammad Ali and Maulana Shaukat Ali start in India in 1919?
15. When Mahatma Gandhi called off the Non-Cooperation Movement due to the Chauri Chaura incident, a faction of the Indian National Congress wanted to continue it, who were known as the 'No-Changers', while another faction, known as the 'Pro-Changers', wanted to end the legislature boycott and contest elections. This led to a rift among the members. C.R. Das and Motilal Nehru, who were Pro-Changers, resigned from the party and formed a political party of their own. Which party thus came into being?
16. Mahatma Gandhi's indefinite fast against the proposal of the Communal Award by British Prime Minister Ramsay MacDonald came to an end with the signing of the Poona Pact with B.R. Ambedkar. As an immediate

outcome of the Poona Pact, what did Mahatma Gandhi form in 1932 for the abolition of untouchability and the uplift of the Dalit class?

17. This prominent Indian freedom activist was termed the 'conscience keeper of Gandhi'. When Gandhi led the Dandi March in 1930, he did the same in the Madras Presidency. In the absence of Lord Mountbatten, he served as the last acting Governor General of India after India's Independence. Who am I referring to?

18. In the 1960s, when India was on the verge of a mass famine, this Indian geneticist, along with American agronomist Norman Borlaug and other scientists, developed High Yielding Variety seeds of wheat. This development led to the Green Revolution in India, and for his contribution to increased agricultural output, he came to be known as 'the father of the Green Revolution in India'. Who is he?

19. In a bid to conserve and protect trees from being felled in Reni village of the Chamoli district in Uttarakhand, which famous nationwide movement did Sundarlal Bahuguna, Gaura Devi, Sudesha Devi, Bachni Devi and Chandi Prasad Bhatt start by hugging the trees when people came to cut them down?

20. Literally translated as 'the followers of the mad path', this socio-religious movement was started in the eighteenth century in Bengal and eastern India under the leadership of Sufi fakir Karim Shah and Tipu Shah. The socio-religious order preached monotheism, non-violence and unity among the various religious sects of society. Later, the followers of the movement

revolted against the oppressive taxations imposed by the British in India. Identify the movement.

ANSWERS

1. The Self-Respect Movement.
2. The breaking of the salt laws by Gandhi during the Civil Disobedience Movement.
3. Dr B.R. Ambedkar.
4. The Cripps Mission, 1942.
5. Atal Bihari Vajpayee.
6. Shyamlal Gupta.
7. 'Jana Gana Mana'.
8. *The Discovery of India* by Pandit Jawaharlal Nehru.
9. Raja Ram Mohan Roy.
10. The Kuka Movement (also known as the Namdhari Movement).
11. The Constitution of India.
12. The Temple Entry Movement.
13. V.D. Savarkar.
14. The Khilafat Movement.
15. The Swaraj Party.
16. The All India Anti-Untouchability League.
17. C. Rajagopalachari.
18. Dr Mankombu Sambasivan Swaminathan.
19. The Chipko Movement.
20. The Pagal Panthis Movement.

DID YOU KNOW?

During the Second World War, the Japanese army had occupied the Andaman and Nicobar islands. Subhas Chandra Bose, who led the Indian National Army in alliance with the Japanese, hoisted the national flag at Port Blair on 30 December 1945. Recently, there has been a growing demand for the Andaman and Nicobar islands to be renamed 'Shaheed and Swaraj Islands' as a tribute to Netaji.

5

FACETS OF THE INDIAN FREEDOM STRUGGLE

1. One of the outstanding leaders of the Revolt of 1857 was Rani Laxmi Bai, who assumed the leadership of the sepoys at Jhansi. The contention of Laxmi Bai with the British started when Lord Dalhousie refused to allow her adopted son to succeed the throne after the death of her husband, Raja Gangadhar Rao. Moreover, Lord Dalhouise annexed Jhansi under a policy he had devised during his tenure as Governor General. Which policy was this?
2. In the early twentieth century, which mass sociopolitical movement did the Arya Samaj start with the aim of reconverting those individuals back to Hinduism who had earlier converted to other religions? Under this movement, Dayanand Saraswati worked extensively on the aspect of Hindu unification and development.
3. Gopal Krishna Gokhale founded the Servants of Indian Society in 1905 to overthrow British rule and work for the development of various important aspects of Indian

society. The organization started the publication of an English newspaper from 1911. Identify the newspaper, which is currently considered one of the largest-selling broadsheet English dailies in central India.

4. Which Hindu religious and spiritual movement works on the basic principle of 'Service to Jiva is service to Shiva' (Service to Man is service to God)?
5. Which Parsee social reformer founded the Seva Sadan, a social reform and humanitarian organization in 1885, which took care of women who were exploited and discarded by society?
6. Who is known as 'the father of Marathi journalism', who started the first Marathi newspaper named *Darpan* in 1832, wherein he wrote extensively about Brahminical orthodoxy and tried to bring about a sense of patriotism and social awareness among the masses?
7. Which sociopolitical organization did Mahadev Govind Ranade and others form in 1867, with the objective of serving as a bridge and mediating body between the British government and the people?
8. To express the commitment of the Indian freedom struggle to give the women of India their due status and respect in national life, the Congress session of 1890 was addressed by the first female graduate from India. Identify the personality, who was also a trained physician in Western medicine.
9. Ideologically, the pre-Independent Indian National Congress had two factions. The first was known as the Moderates, who believed in peaceful and non-violent

means to achieve freedom, and included members such as Gandhi, Dadabhai Naoroji and Rash Behari Ghosh. The other faction was known as the Extremists, who undertook aggressive and violent means, and included members such as Lala Lajpat Rai, Bal Gangadhar Tilak and Bipin Chandra Pal. The methodology of the Moderates was widely known as 'the three P's'. What did they stand for?

10. The influence of the Swadeshi Movement was not just confined to the rejection of foreign goods. Its influence was visible in restoring the value of Indian art and painting as well. During this period, which famous artist created the Indian Society of Oriental Art, along with his brother, to revive and develop Indian art over Victorian, in India?

11. Considered 'the father of modern Indian chemistry', which prominent nationalist and academician revolutionized the Indian industry during British rule by dedicating himself to the spread of a scientific temper among Indians and establishing the first pharmaceutical company, Bengal Chemical & Pharmaceutical Works?

12. A socialist political leader and a noted freedom fighter of India, he was imprisoned for two years for writing an article titled 'Satyagraha Now' in Gandhi's newspaper, *Harijan*. One of his major writings, *Marx, Gandhi and Socialism*, left a lasting impression on Indian political literature. In his efforts to provide assistance to Indian farmers, he also founded the Hind Kisan Panchayat. Who was he?

13. Founded by Sisir Ghosh and Moti Lal Ghosh, and

named after the wife of Hari Narayan Ghosh, which oldest daily in South Asia was started in 1868, wherein several fiery articles were published to arouse patriotic sentiment?

14. Born to Trailokyanath Bose and Lakshmipriya Devi, who became the youngest Indian revolutionist to be hanged during the Indian freedom movement for his involvement in the attempt to assassinate Magistrate Kingsford, which, however, accidently took the lives of two innocent British women?

15. A notable educationist and leader of the freedom struggle, Madan Mohan Malviya, realizing the importance of newspapers to educate the masses about nationalism and freedom, started several newspapers such as *Abhyudaya*, *Hindustan* and *Indian Union*. Apart from these, which educational institute did he establish, along with Annie Besant?

16. As the Swadeshi movement spread throughout the country, in the south this activist played a pioneering role in kindling nationalism and patriotism with his fiery poems and songs in the Tamil language. He is popularly known as the 'Tamil Mahakavi'. Identify the Tamil writer and poet.

17. This Indian Independence activist became the president of the Indian National Congress in 1925 and later the governor of the United Provinces (now Uttar Pradesh). The British government also awarded her with the prestigious Kaisar-i-Hind medal for her stellar work during the plague epidemic in India. Known for her love for poetry, her two collections of poems are

named *The Golden Threshold* and *The Feather of the Dawn.* Identify her.

18. Lala Harkishen Lal was an Indian industrialist, politician and freedom activist who played a pivotal role in the Punjab province in promoting Swadeshi. In a bid to bring the essence of Swadeshi to the field of business and industry, which famous institution did he co-found, along with personalities such as Lala Lajpat Rai and Dyal Singh Majithia?

19. An active member of the Anushilan Samiti, this Indian nationalist was probably the first Indian revolutionary who went abroad, to Paris, to learn the technique of assembling picric acid bombs and military techniques from exiled Russian revolutionaries. Later, he opened a secret bomb factory in Calcutta (now Kolkata) named Anusilonee Somitee. Identify the forgotten hero who was a principal co-accused, along with Aurobindo Ghose, in the Alipore Bomb Case of 1908.

20. In 1906, while studying law in London, which Indian independent activist compiled a volume titled *Mazzini Charitra*, a vivid translation of the Italian revolutionary Giuseppe Mazzini's writings into Marathi and Hindi, highlighting Mazzini's guerrilla warfare and techniques of secret societies, which he used for the unification of Italy?

ANSWERS

1. The Doctrine of Lapse.
2. The Shuddhi Movement.
3. *The Hitavada*.
4. The Ramakrishna Movement.
5. Behramji M. Malabari.
6. Balshastri Jambhekar.
7. Poona Sarvajanik Sabha.
8. Kadambini Ganguly.
9. Prayer. Petition. Protest.
10. Abanindranath Tagore, along with his brother Gaganendranath Tagore.
11. Prafulla Chandra Roy.
12. Ram Manohar Lohia.
13. *Amrita Bazar Patrika*, named after Amritamoyee.
14. Khudiram Bose.
15. Banaras Hindu University, formerly known as Central Hindu College.
16. Subramania Bharati.
17. Sarojini Naidu, the first female governor of an Indian state.
18. Punjab National Bank.
19. Hemchandra Kanungo Das.
20. V.D. Savarkar.

DID YOU KNOW?

The University Grants Commission (UGC), a statutory body, was constituted in 1956 for looking into the standards of higher education in India under the direct recommendation of the University Education Commission, under the chairmanship of Dr Sarvepalli Radhakrishnan, a former President of India. This was the first commission formed for higher education in Independent India.

6

HISTORICAL POTPOURRI

1. Malayapuram Singaravelu Chettiar was a major leader of the Indian Independence movement in the south. A lawyer by profession, he played a significant role in the inclusion of labourers in the freedom movement. He was associated with the first trade unions in India. With his ideology of anti-capitalism, he is credited with starting the celebration of which occasion in India?
2. A prominent Indian freedom fighter and politician, she is credited with founding the All India Mahila Congress in 1940. She came to the forefront of the Indian Independence struggle during the Quit India Movement. On 14 August 1947, she sang 'Vande Mataram' in the Independence session of the Constituent Assembly, minutes before Jawaharlal Nehru delivered his famous 'Tryst with Destiny' speech. Identify the famous personality.
3. A key Indian revolutionary, radical activist, political theorist and a stalwart of communism in India, he was the founder of the Mexican Communist Party and the

Communist Party of India (CPI). It was during his stay in New York that he developed his interest in Marxist ideology. He also served as the editor of the globally acclaimed communist journal, *Vanguard*. During the period of the national freedom movement, he unapologetically advocated the use of armed struggle against the British. The first idea to form a Constituent Assembly in India for framing a written constitution was also conceived by him. Identify this personality, who wore many hats in Indian history.

4. Bhagwan Ahir, an army pensioner, was a small-time peasant activist from Gorakhpur village. While conducting peaceful satyagraha in the area, the British police beat him up without any provocation. This incident flared up nationalist sentiments and anger across the villages of Gorakhpur. Which historic event happened next?

5. In a different aspect of civil disobedience in India against British rule, the concept of which form of satyagraha was formulated and launched by Bapuji Aney, wherein he mobilized thousands of Adivasi peasants in Vidharbha. His ideology started to spread and satyagraha eventually engulfed the whole of India. For his stellar contribution to the cause of Indian freedom, he was often referred to as 'Loknayak'. Which form of satyagraha did he start?

6. Born to a Syrian Christian family in Calicut in 1921, this personality was deeply touched by the discouraging state of monopoly in milk production during his later years. In 1970, he launched 'Operation Flood' to make India self-sufficient in dairy production using

scientific and innovative ways, thus bringing in the 'White Revolution'. Identify the famous personality who is credited with establishing Amul in Gujarat.

7. Lovingly known as 'Lokpriya', or the beloved of the people, this Indian Independence activist went on to become the first chief minister of Assam. An undeterred nationalist and Gandhian supporter, he played a key role in standing up to the grouping system of the British Cabinet Mission, wherein the British arbitrarily divided Assam and most of the Northeast as a Muslim-majority state. It was due to his revolutionary activities and heroic leadership that Assam and her people were rescued from the conspiracy of the British. Identify the personality.

8. The court martial of three stalwarts of the Azad Hind Fauj, namely Shah Nawaz Khan, Prem Sahgal and Gurbaksh Singh Dhillon, who were officers in the Indian National Army of British India, due to anti-British activity during their campaign in Burma (now Myanmar) and Imphal, along with the Japanese army, gave rise to a landmark mass movement and agitation in the country. This agitation against the British is historically seen as one of the most important factors that contributed to India's freedom. Where were the Indian National Army trials held?

9. Which socio-religious reform movement based its ideologies on monotheism, the uplift of women, and the abolition of caste discrimination and religious orthodoxy, and was founded by Atmaram Pandurang, along with Mahadev Govind Ranade, in 1867?

10. In a major episode of the Civil Disobedience Movement in India, the Kunbi-Patidar landowning peasants and the lower-caste farmers of Gujarat started a satyagraha in 1928 against the oppression of the upper-caste zamindars and the British government for hiking the land revenue by 22 per cent. It was during this satyagraha that Vallabhbhai Patel got the title of 'Sardar' conferred on him by the local farmers for leading the satyagraha. Which satyagraha was this?
11. Currently known as the 'August Kranti Park' in central Mumbai, it was from this historical place that Mahatma Gandhi gave his Quit India speech on 8 August 1942, announcing that the British leave India immediately or face mass agitations in the country. In his speech, Gandhi gave India the iconic 'Karo ya Maro' ('Do or Die') slogan. What was the original name of the park, which was initially used by cattle owners to bathe their cows?
12. This term was coined by parliamentarian Dr Laxmi Mall Singhvi, which literally means 'caretaker of the people'. The first Bill to introduce this office in India was laid out in the Lok Sabha by former law minister of India Shanti Bhushan, way back in 1968. What am I speaking of?
13. Yusuf Meherally played a major role in India's struggle for Independence, where he organized several peasant movements and trade unions against the British. At the age of 39, Meherally became the mayor of Bombay, the first socialist to be elected to the post. However, he is best known for coining two iconic slogans that defined India's Independence struggle. One was 'Quit India'; which is the other?

14. Popularly known as 'Comrade Sak', this personality was born in India on 28 March 1874, and later moved to England in 1905. He went on to become a two-time member of the British Parliament and is known as a titan of the Communist movement in Great Britain. A formidable orator, he gave fiery speeches in Britain against the tyrannical policies of the British in India, which managed to gather huge global attention. In 1936, when he died, Jawaharlal Nehru referred to him as the 'most important nationalist figure outside the country'. Who am I referring to?

15. He championed freedom of the press and social harmony, and extensively argued for assembly status for the National Capital Territory of Delhi. It was Swami Shraddhanand and Mahatma Gandhi who conferred upon him the title of 'Friend of the Nation' for his stellar contribution to politics and the Indian freedom struggle. Identify this personality, who started a newspaper called *Rozana Tej* with help from the Arya Samaj.

16. Hansa Jivraj Mehta, a prominent freedom fighter and an activist of women's rights, was appointed as the Indian representative to the United Nations Human Rights Commission in 1947 by the then Prime Minister Jawaharlal Nehru. She was single-handedly responsible for amending a critical feature of the Universal Declaration of Human Rights adopted by the United Nations General Assembly in 1948, which brought a true sense of gender equality in the declaration. Which crucial amendment was made in Article 1 of the declaration at her behest?

17. Born as Edith Ellen Gray, she was an Englishwoman who fought for Indian Independence. As a young girl, she fell in love with and married Jatindra Mohan Sengupta, who was an Indian revolutionary. She took active part in the Non-Cooperation Movement along with her husband. This lesser-known freedom fighter was later elected as the president of the Indian National Congress at its 47th session in Calcutta. Which name is she more popularly known as?

18. She is remembered as one of India's most dynamic freedom fighters and a champion of social welfare and women's rights. Married off at the tender age of 8, she later withdrew from the marriage and set sail for the cause of India's freedom struggle. During this time, she formed the Andhra Mahila Sabha and the Central Social Welfare Board for the emancipation of society. Later, at the age of 44, she married C.D. Deshmukh, the first Indian governor of the Reserve Bank of India. Her autobiography, *Chintaman and I*, paints a vivid picture of the events of her life. Identify her.

19. Born on 8 October 1877 in erstwhile Orissa, he is also known as the 'Gandhi of Orissa'. Netaji Subhas Chandra Bose referred to him as the 'father of the national movement of Orissa'. Due to his several notable contributions to the freedom struggle, social reforms, political activism, journalism and literature, he earned the title of 'Utkalamami' (Jewel of Utkal, or Orissa). Identify this freedom fighter, who had a lasting impact on the history of this eastern state.

20. Known as the 'Iron lady of Bengal', she was probably

the first Bengali woman to pick up arms against the British. She led several anti-British campaigns under the guidance of Surya Sen of Anushilan Samiti. She was one of the main forces behind the Chittagong uprising. She sacrificed her life by ingesting cyanide during a fierce gunfight with the British troops while torching the Pahartali European Club in 1932 to avenge the Jalalabad massacre. Identify the legendary revolutionist of India.

ANSWERS

1. Celebration of May Day or Labour Day on 1 May.
2. Sucheta Kriplani.
3. Manabendra Nath Roy.
4. The angry villagers killed 22 policemen, which led to the Chauri Chaura incident.
5. Forest Satyagraha.
6. Verghese Kurien.
7. Gopinath Bordoloi.
8. The Red Fort. They are also known as the Red Fort Trials.
9. Prarthana Samaj.
10. Bardoli Satyagraha.
11. Gowalia Tank Maidan.
12. Lokpal.
13. 'Simon Go Back'.
14. Shapurji Saklatvala.
15. Rati Ram Deshbandhu Gupta.

16. 'All men are born free and equal' was amended to 'All human beings are born free and equal'.
17. Nellie Sengupta.
18. Durgabai Deshmukh.
19. Gopabandhu Das.
20. Pritilata Waddedar.

DID YOU KNOW?

A young college girl from Gujarat named Usha Mehta ran a secret radio station named 'Congress Radio', which functioned for a total of 88 days during the Quit India Movement. The radio station would broadcast speeches by famous leaders such as Gandhi, Nehru and Ram Manohar Lohia, and play patriotic songs to ignite the spirit of nationalism among the masses. In 1998, she was conferred the Padma Vibhushan award.

7

SACRIFICES GALORE

1. Affectionately known as 'Bi Amma', she was one of the first female Muslim freedom fighters to take active part in the Independence movement in the mid-nineteenth century. Throughout her life, she campaigned for Hindu-Muslim unity and harmony, which she believed was essential for freedom from the British. Her sons, Shaukat Ali and Mohammad Ali, went on to play a pivotal role in the Khilafat Movement. Identify her.

2. The Battle of Khongjom in Manipur is regarded as one of the fiercest battles against the British in the history of India. It all began with the disintegration of unity among the princes of Manipur after the death of Maharaja Chandrakirti in 1890. The British saw it as an opportunity and attacked Manipur in a bid to arrest the then king, Maharaja Kulchand Singh, and take full control of the state. This triggered the Battle of Khongjom in 1891. During the battle, a brave soldier of the Manipuri kingdom took the centre stage and led the attack against the better-equipped British

army. Even though the Manipuri soldier lost the battle, his valour left a lasting mark on the pages of Indian history. Name the soldier.

3. Due to his involvement in the Ghadar Conspiracy, this Indian revolutionary was sentenced to jail and was briefly imprisoned at the Cellular Jail in the Andaman and Nicobar islands. While in jail, he wrote the book *Bandi Jeevan*, an account of the revolutionary activities in India during that time. He was jailed again due to his involvement in the Kakori Conspiracy. Identify the famous revolutionary, who was also a mentor to later revolutionaries such as Bhagat Singh and Chandra Shekhar Azad.
4. A fiery Parsee lawyer and a stalwart of the Indian National Congress, he organized the Civil Disobedience Movement in the Bombay province in 1930. He first came to public attention in 1928 for his vehement protest against and exposure of the Bombay Backbay Reclamation financial scandal by the British government. Identify him.
5. He is a lesser-known freedom activist from Kerala. A brilliant scholar and academician, he began working for the cause of the freedom struggle due to his close association with Jayaprakash Narayan. During the Quit India Movement, he was the brain behind the Keezhariyur Bomb Case, where he oversaw the making of bombs to be used against the British. He is known as 'the architect of the Quit India Movement in Malabar'. Identify him.
6. This eighteenth-century warrior king was one of

the earliest freedom fighters of India, who valiantly fought for the country and refused to bow down to the British. One of the most significant victories during his rule was the 'Cotiote War', where he defeated Arthur Wellesley, the first Duke of Wellington. Due to his valiant crushing of most of the native warlords and British generals, he is lovingly known at the 'Kerala Simham' or 'the Lion of Kerala'. Identify this forgotten hero.

7. Benoy Basu, Badal Gupta and Dinesh Gupta were three young revolutionists involved in the assassination of Colonel N.S. Simpson of the Indian Imperial Police for his brutal oppression of political prisoners. A fierce gunfight broke out. However, the British police soon outnumbered them. Refusing to be arrested, Benoy and Dinesh shot themselves with their own revolvers, while Badal consumed a tablet of potassium cyanide. The martyrdom and sacrifice of the three bravehearts inspired further revolutionary activity in India. This incident, which was also known as 'the Corridor Warfare', took place in which prominent structure in Bengal?

8. Which prominent freedom fighter and revolutionist worked as an extra in two British films directed by Alexander Korda—*Elephant Boy* (1937) and *The Four Feathers* (1939)?

9. In his autobiography *The Story of My Experiments with Truth*, Mahatma Gandhi describes this person as '...but ______ was as the Ganges. One could have a refreshing bath in the holy river. The Himalaya was unscalable, and one could not easily launch forth on the sea, but

the Ganges invited one to its bosom. It was a joy to be on it with a boat and an oar.' Who is being referred to here?

10. The youth and student community played an important role in the freedom movement in India. To discourage and prevent the participation of the student community in the Civil Disobedience Movement of 1930, the British administration in Assam issued a circular that forbade students from joining the movement or any matter of active politics in the state. This led to widespread protest and agitation in Assam against the draconian policies of the British. It eventually resulted in the establishment of indigenous educational institutions such as Kamrup Academy, Sivsagar Vidyapith and Barpeta Vidyapith. What was the name of the circular issued?

11. Founded by Aruna Roy, Nikhil Dey and Shankar Singh in 1987, Mazdoor Kisan Shakti Sangathan is an association for the empowerment of labourers and farmers in Rajasthan. In a bid to bring about transparency in the village accounts of Beawar in Ajmer, the sangathan began a forty-day sit-in protest against the state government in 1996. What was the historic outcome of the protest?

12. Written by Pandit Vanshidhar Shukla and composed by freedom fighter Ram Singh Thakuri, this iconic song was banned in India by the British for being 'seditious'. Identify this song, which currently serves as the regimental quick march of the Indian Army.

13. *Purab Ki Awaz* is a Hindi translated movie based on the

life and activities of a young female freedom fighter from Assam who was shot dead by the police while leading a procession to hoist the national flag at a local police station in Gohpur in Assam during the Quit India Movement. Her contribution to and sacrifice for the country remains a source of inspiration to many. Identify the braveheart who died at the young age of 17.

14. In 1909, while studying in London, this young Indian revolutionary assassinated William Hutt Curzon Wyllie of the British army, the political aide to the secretary of state for India during that time. This assassination is considered to be one of the first acts of armed revolution during the Indian freedom struggle. He was later arrested, tried and sentenced to death by the British government. Identify this famous personality, who was an inspiration to later leaders and revolutionaries such as Bhagat Singh and Chandra Shekhar Azad.

15. Under the patronage of the Indian revolutionary fighter and lawyer Shyamji Krishna Varma, a student hostel was opened in London for Indian students studying in Britain. This hostel rapidly became one of the most prominent hubs of political and revolutionary activism for Indians. For a brief period, it also served as the organizational headquarters of the Indian Home Rule Society. It was from this hostel that the nationalist journal *The Indian Sociologist* was published, which criticized British oppression of India. Identify this historic residence in London.

16. A prominent member of the Naujawan Bharat Sabha,

this unsung national hero helped in the escape of Bhagat Singh, Batukeshwar Dutt and Durgawati Devi from the Mauzang House in Lahore. He died due to force-feeding during his imprisonment in the Cellular Jail. Identify this revolutionary, whose statue can be seen today in front of the Cellular Jail in the Andaman islands.

17. During the Indian freedom movement, which groups were known as the 'Naram Dal' (soft faction) and the 'Garam Dal' (hot faction), signifying the ideologies their activities were based on?

18. Who, along with his close associate Genda Lal Dixit, formed a revolutionary organization called Matrivedi (Altar of the Motherland), which had four departments—secret services, building of a stock of arms, fund collection, and propagation of nationalism and awareness of the organization through literature. Later, he wrote a famous poem titled *Mainpuri Ki Pratigya*, wherein he wrote about the ideologies and activities of Matrivedi, which was formed in Mainpuri, Uttar Pradesh.

19. He acquired the title of 'Senapati', meaning 'commander', for his leadership during the Mulshi Satyagraha, a movement to represent the farmers whose land had been taken by the British government to build the Mulshi dam in the Pune district of Maharashtra in 1920. Identify the popular freedom fighter from Maharashtra, who later became the first person to hoist the Indian national flag in Pune after India's Independence.

20. Nicknamed 'Mother Teresa of Western Orissa', she was a prominent freedom fighter, who took active part in the Quit India Movement. After India gained Independence, she dedicated her life to social causes, such as leprosy eradication, the improvement of prison conditions, the welfare of orphans and the uplift of the downtrodden. Identify her.

ANSWERS

1. Abadi Bano Begum.
2. Paona Brajabashi.
3. Sachindra Nath Sanyal.
4. Khurshed Nariman, after whom Nariman Point in Mumbai is named.
5. Dr K.B. Menon.
6. Pazhassi Raja.
7. The Writers' Building, the secretariat building of the state government of West Bengal. Later, a commemorative structure of Benoy, Badal and Dinesh was constructed in front of the Writers' Building.
8. Udham Singh.
9. Gopal Krishna Gokhale.
10. The Cunningham Circular, named after J.R. Cunningham, the then director of the Education department.
11. The enactment of the Right to Information Act in the Parliament of India.
12. 'Qadam Qadam Badhaye Ja'.
13. Kanaklata Barua.

14. Madan Lal Dhingra.
15. India House.
16. Mahavir Singh.
17. The two factions of the Indian National Congress. The Moderates, led by Gopal Krishna Gokhale, were known as the 'Naram Dal', while the Extremists, led by Bal Gangadhar Tilak, were known as the 'Garam Dal'.
18. Ram Prasad Bismil.
19. Pandurang Mahadev Bapat.
20. Parbati Giri.

DID YOU KNOW?

In a small village in the Sangli district of Maharashtra, there exists a memorial of all Indian martyrs during the freedom movement. However, the memorial does not have any statues, structures or inscriptions. Instead, in the name of every martyr, a tree has been planted. This unique memorial is known as Kranti Van. A farmer named Sampatrao Pawar owns the memorial.

8

BOOKS AND AUTHORS

Identify the famous Indian authors of the following classic works written during the colonial period.

1. *Hind Swaraj*
2. *We or Our Nationhood Defined*
3. *Gandhi vs Lenin*
4. *India Wins Freedom*
5. *Letters from Russia*
6. *India Today*
7. *India in Transition*
8. *Why I Am an Atheist*
9. *The Golden Threshold*
10. *Vande Mataram*
11. *Unhappy India*
12. *Hints for Self-Culture*
13. *A Voice for Freedom*
14. *Love and Death*

15. *India for Indians*
16. *India Divided*
17. *A Nation in Making*
18. *An Indian Pilgrim*
19. *The Autobiography of an Unknown Indian*
20. *England's Debt to India*

ANSWERS

1. Mahatma Gandhi.
2. M.S. Golwalkar.
3. S.A. Dange.
4. Maulana Abul Kalam Azad.
5. Rabindranath Tagore.
6. R.P. Dutt.
7. M.N. Roy.
8. Bhagat Singh.
9. Sarojini Naidu.
10. Aurobindo Ghose.
11. Lala Lajpat Rai.
12. Lala Har Dayal.
13. Nayantara Sahgal.
14. Aurobindo Ghose.
15. Chittaranjan Das.
16. Dr Rajendra Prasad.
17. Sir Surendranath Banerjee.
18. Subhas Chandra Bose.

19. Nirad C. Chaudhuri.
20. Lala Lajpat Rai.

DID YOU KNOW?

The Great Indian Novel is a satirical novel by Shashi Tharoor on the Indian Independence movement. He narrates events by choosing the characters of the novel from the epic Mahabharata. A unique style of historical narrative, the book is an interesting juxtaposition of Indian mythology and the historical events of the Indian freedom struggle.

9

NEWSPAPERS, JOURNALS AND MAGAZINES

Identify the pioneers and founders of the following newspapers, journals and magazines started during the colonial rule in India.

1. *The Bengalee* (1862)
2. The *Pioneer* (1865)
3. *Kesari* (1881)
4. *Voice of India* (1883)
5. *Indian Opinion* (1903)
6. *Yugantar Patrika* (1906)
7. *Modern Review* (1907)
8. *Bande Mataram* (1909)
9. *The Bombay Chronicle* (1913)
10. *Commonweal* (1914)
11. *Sambad Kaumudi* (1819)

12. *The Independent* (1919)
13. *Sakal* (1932)
14. *Nava Bharat* (1934)
15. *The Indian P.E.N.* (1934)
16. *Inquilab* (1937)
17. *Karmyogin* (1909)
18. *Pratap* (1913)
19. *Aaj* (1920)
20. *Lokmat* (1930)

ANSWERS

1. Girish Chandra Ghosh.
2. George Allen.
3. Bal Gangadhar Tilak.
4. Dadabhai Naoroji.
5. Mahatma Gandhi.
6. Barindra Kumar Ghosh, Abhinash Bhattacharya and Bhupendranath Dutt.
7. Ramanand Chatterjee.
8. Bhikaji Cama.
9. Sir Pherozeshah Mehta.
10. Annie Besant.
11. Raja Ram Mohan Roy.
12. Motilal Nehru.
13. N.B. Parulekar.
14. Ramgopal Maheshwari.

15. Sophia Wadia.
16. Khalid Ansari.
17. Sri Aurobindo.
18. Ganesh Shankar Vidyarthi.
19. Shiv Prasad Gupta.
20. Seth Govind Das and D.P. Mishra.

DID YOU KNOW?

In 1920, B.R. Ambedkar started the Marathi newspaper *Mook Nayak* (The Mute Hero), which was the first newspaper in India exclusively started to voice the problems and issues of Dalits, the untouchables and the depressed classes of society. Later, in 1927, he started another Marathi fortnightly, *Bahishkrit Bharat* (India Ostracized), for the same purpose.

10

EARLY POLITICAL ASSOCIATIONS

Identify the founders of the following early associations, which played pivotal roles in gaining India its freedom.

1. Bangabhasha Prakashika Sabha (1836)
2. Landholders' Society (1836)
3. British India Society (1843)
4. British India Association (1852)
5. Bombay Association (1852)
6. London India Committee (1862)
7. East India Association (1866)
8. National Indian Association (1867)
9. Indian Society (1872)
10. Indian Association (1876)
11. Poona Sarvajanik Sabha (1876)
12. Indian National Society (1883)
13. Indian National Conference (1884)

14. Bombay Presidency Association (1885)
15. United India Patriotic Association (1888)
16. All India Trade Union Congress (1920)
17. All India Communist Party (1924)
18. Khudai Khidmatgar (1928)
19. All India Kisan Sabha (1936)
20. Radical Democratic Party (1940)

ANSWERS

1. Raja Ram Mohan Roy.
2. Dwarkanath Tagore.
3. William Adams.
4. Dwarkanath Tagore and Debendranath Tagore.
5. Jagannath Shankar Sheth.
6. C.P. Subbiah Mudaliar.
7. Dadabhai Naoroji.
8. Mary Carpenter.
9. Anand Mohan Bose.
10. Sir Surendranath Banerjee and Anand Mohan Bose.
11. Mahadev Govind Ranade, Ganesh Vasudeo Joshi and S.H. Chiplunkar.
12. Sisir Chandra Bose.
13. Sir Surendranath Banerjee.
14. Pherozeshah Mehta, K.T. Telang and Badruddin Tyabji.
15. Sir Syed Ahmed Khan.
16. Narayan Malhar Joshi.

17. Satyabhakta.
18. Khan Abdul Ghaffar Khan.
19. Sahajanand Saraswati and N.G. Ranga.
20. M.N. Roy.

DID YOU KNOW?

The Naujawan Bharat Sabha was an association founded by Bhagat Singh, which was based on his socialistic ideology and was secular in its outlook and character. It was the public face of the Hindustan Socialist Republican Association. Due to the involvement of the members of the Naujawan Bharat Sabha in the J.P. Saunders assassination case, the British government in 1929 banned the association.

11

REVOLUTIONARY HISTORY–I

1. Moments before his execution, when the jail authorities asked Bhagat Singh to get ready for the noose, it is claimed that he courteously said, 'Wait a while, a revolutionary is talking to another revolutionary', as he continued to read a book. After a few more minutes of reading, he threw the book up in the air and said, 'Let's go.' Which book was Bhagat Singh reading?
2. Which 1967 blockbuster Hindi film was based on Lal Bahadur Shastri's iconic slogan '*Jai Jawan Jai Kisan*', which showed patriotism for the country and the essence of agriculture?
3. In a lesser-known but glorious chapter of the Indian freedom struggle, two Deobandi leaders, Maulana Mahmood Hasan and Ubaidullah Sindhi, started a movement with the onset of the First World War to mobilize the support of the governments of Germany, Afghanistan and Turkey in organizing a full-fledged revolt in India to overthrow British rule. Identify the famous revolution, which interestingly gets its name

from the material on which the leaders used to write their secret letters.

4. This firebrand revolutionary from Bengal was the principal leader of the secret revolutionary society Yugantar. Involved in the Howrah-Sibpur and the Indo-German Conspiracy cases, he created a name for himself during the freedom movement. Interestingly, the government of Bengal awarded him a silver shield for barehandedly killing a man-eating tiger in his native village, thus earning him the title of 'Tiger' in Bengali. Who am I speaking of?
5. Martyred at the age of 19, this Grewal Jat Sikh freedom fighter was an active member of the Ghadar Party. He was regarded as the real inspiration and guru of Bhagat Singh. Singh would always carry his picture in his pocket. Once, while speaking to his mother, Singh pointed to the photograph and said, 'Dear mother, this is my hero, friend and companion.' Who was he?
6. Born as Margaret Elizabeth Noble, this Irish woman later moved to India under the inspiration and association of Swami Vivekananda. After taking the vows of Brahmacharya, she was given a name that she is more popularly known as. Identify this famous social worker, whose epitaph reads, 'Here lies ________ ________, who gave her all to India.'
7. A rather lesser-known historic event, which took place on 29 July 1911, was reported by the famous British newspaper *The Englishman* (now *The Statesman*) as '________ ________ has succeeded in what the Congress and the Swadeshiwallas have failed to do so

far to explode the myth that Britishers are unbeatable in any sphere of life'. Fill in the blanks.

8. Bakshi Jagabandhu, the commander of the Khordha army, is considered one of the earliest freedom fighters in Indian history. Which armed rebellion was carried out under his leadership against the British East India Company's exploitative land-revenue policy in Orissa in 1817?

9. Locally known as the 'Punjabi Monument', this structure is modelled on the kripan (dagger) carried by the Sikhs. Jawaharlal Nehru inaugurated it in 1952 near Budge Budge in present-day West Bengal. This monument was built to commemorate which historic incident during the Indian freedom struggle?

10. He was born in the Azamgarh district of Uttar Pradesh. A bookbinder by profession, he was an active freedom fighter in the Rebellion of 1857. He also used to secretly distribute leaflets, pamphlets and coded messages to fellow freedom fighters. Later, when the British came to know about his revolutionary activities, he was hanged on 7 July 1857 in Patna, Bihar. Who was he?

11. Born in Chennimalai, Tamil Nadu, this notable freedom fighter founded the Desa Bandhu Youth Association and led several protests against the British. In one such protest in 1932, he was brutally assaulted by British officials for carrying the national flag. Despite being on the verge of dying, he clung to the flag and ensured that it did not touch the ground. This heroic incident gained him the title of 'Kodi Kaatha', or the Protector

of the Flag. Identify this lesser-known hero.

12. This legendary social reformer and freedom activist is best known for her multifaceted accomplishments and immense contribution to India's cultural and social fabric. In 1926, she became the first Indian woman to contest for a legislative seat, from Madras (now Chennai). She was the first Indian woman to be arrested during Gandhi's Salt Satyagraha, when she entered the Bombay Stock Exchange to sell swadeshi salt. After Independence, she was one of the founding figures of the National School of Drama and the Sangeet Natak Akademi. Identify her.

13. For which specific purpose did the Government of India appoint Justice Manoj Kumar as the chairperson of the Mukherjee Commission in 1999?

14. Spread across 1,100 acres, this piece of land near Johannesburg was donated by Hermann Kallenbach to Mahatma Gandhi for setting up a cooperative colony for the establishment of a swadeshi ashram in South Africa in 1910. By what name was the ashram known, which was named after an author Gandhi was deeply inspired by?

15. Mahatma Gandhi was declared the runner-up for the title of *TIME* magazine's 'Person of the Century' in 1999, which is conducted every hundred years. Who topped the selection?

16. One of the pioneering leaders of the Indian freedom movement, his name used to be famously referred to as 'Surrender Not' by the British for his indomitable spirit. How do we better know 'Surrender Not'?

17. Popularly known as 'Krantisinh' (revolutionary lion), this Indian freedom fighter founded a parallel government against British rule in the Satara district of Maharashtra, which was called 'Prati Sarkar'. This was short-lived (1943–45), but worked extensively for village community development and conducting frugal Gandhi Marriages. Identify the personality.

18. During the later part of the Indian freedom movement, which incident did the then viceroy of India, Lord Wavell, describe as 'an edge of a volcano', referring to the mounting mass pressure on the British government's foundations in India?

19. In the early 1900s, freedom fighter Lokmanya Bal Gangadhar Tilak and Parsee businessman Sir Ratan Jamshedji Tata conceived an idea of a local store to promote the manufacture, sale and use of Swadeshi goods across the country, keeping up with the ideologies of the Gandhian Swadeshi Movement. Which popular store thus came into being?

20. On 1 February 1963, the Government of India decided to officially declare the Indian peacock as the national bird. The decision was taken after considering the views of the state governments and the opinions expressed in the press. However, the Indian peacock was not the first choice. The review committee had to change the choice to the Indian peacock, as the first sounded too similar to an expletive. Which bird was this?

ANSWERS

1. *State and Revolution* by Vladimir Lenin.
2. *Upkar*.
3. The Silk Letter Movement.
4. Jatindranath Mukherjee. He earned the nickname Bagha Jatin.
5. Kartar Singh Sarabha.
6. Sister Nivedita.
7. Mohun Bagan. In 1911, the football club Mohun Bagan defeated the East Yorkshire Regiment, an elite branch of the British army, in an unprecedentedly attended football match in Calcutta. After the win, it aroused greater nationalist sentiment across the state.
8. Paika Rebellion.
9. In memory of the 20 Sikhs who were killed by the Indian Imperial Police in the Komagata Maru incident in 1914. *Komagata Maru* was a steamer carrying 376 immigrants from India, who were denied entry to Canada. The ship was turned back to India and, when it reached the Indian shore in Calcutta, the police opened fire.
10. Peer Ali Khan.
11. Tiruppur Kumaran.
12. Kamaladevi Chattopadhyay.
13. To probe the death of Subhas Chandra Bose.
14. Tolstoy Farm.
15. Albert Einstein.
16. Sir Surendranath Banerjee.
17. Nana Patil.

18. INA trials, 1945–46.
19. The Bombay Swadeshi Co-Op Stores Co Ltd. It is now known as the Bombay Stores.
20. The great Indian bustard.

DID YOU KNOW?

In 1921, Kosuri Venkata Ratnam from Andhra Pradesh met Mahatma Gandhi in Wardha, Maharasthra. During this meeting, Gandhi suggested that Ratnam make pens from indigenous materials. This led to the creation of the lesser-known but historic Ratnam Pen Works company—which made India's first swadeshi fountain pen. It is now sold under the name 'Ratnamson Pens'.

12

NOTES, QUOTES AND ANECDOTES

Identify the personalities behind the famous quotes and the historical backgrounds around it.

1. 'I declare that the blows struck at me today will be the last nails in the coffin of the British rule in India.'
2. 'As pure as crystal, as brave as a lion and the most perfect man in the political field.'
3. 'If the deaf are to hear, the sound has to be very loud.'
4. 'I am proud to have the honour of laying down my humble life for my country.'
5. 'Give me blood and I will give you freedom.'
6. 'We have now an open conspiracy to free this country from foreign rule, and you, comrades, and all our countrymen and countrywomen are invited to join it.'
7. 'Here is a mantra, a short one that I give you. You may imprint it in your hearts and let every breath of yours give expression to it. The mantra is—do or die.'
8. 'On bended knees I asked for bread and received

a stone instead. India is one vast prison house. I repudiate this law and regard it as my sacred duty to break the mournful monotony of compulsory peace.'

9. 'So long as you do not achieve social liberty, whatever freedom is provided by the law is of no avail to you.'
10. '*Dushman ki goliyon ka hum samna karenge, azad hee rahein hain, azad hee rahenge*' ('We will face the enemy's bullets; we have been free, and we will remain free').

ANSWERS

1. Lala Lajpat Rai.

   He received a severe head injury due to the lathi charge during the protest march against the recommendations of the Simon Commission. He eventually succumbed to his injuries on 17 November 1928. To avenge Lalaji's death, Bhagat Singh and Shivaram Rajguru shot dead a high-profile British police official named John P. Saunders.
2. Mahatma Gandhi.

   In his autobiography *The Story of My Experiments with Truth*, Gandhi defines Gopal Krishna Gokhale as his political guru and mentor during his formative years.
3. Bhagat Singh.

   Bhagat Singh and Batukeshwar Dutt blasted a bomb in the Central Legislative Assembly on 8 April 1929. It was a heroic act done against the implementation of the Defence of India Act 1915, which the British intended to use to curtail nationalist and revolutionary activities in India by empowering the British police in matters related to arrests and trials.

4. Madan Lal Dhingra.

   On being sentenced to death for assassinating Curzon Wyllie, the advisor to the then secretary of state for India.

5. Subhas Chandra Bose.

   While urging the youth of India to join the Indian National Army to fight for India's freedom.

6. Jawaharlal Nehru.

   On officially announcing 'Poorna Swaraj' as the ultimate goal of the Indian National Congress in the Lahore Session, 1929.

7. Mahatma Gandhi.

   In a bid to land the final assault on British rule in India, Gandhi, in his Quit India Movement speech in Mumbai, urged every individual to jump into the movement and uproot colonial rule or die trying. Thus, '*karenge ya marenge*'.

8. Mahatma Gandhi to Lord Irwin.

   On 2 March 1930, Gandhi sent a long letter to the then viceroy of India, Lord Irwin, emphasizing and clarifying the demands for Independence and immediate abolition of all taxes on salt. It was after the rejection of the letter that Gandhi launched the historic 241-mile Salt Satyagraha march to the seashore of Dandi.

9. B.R. Ambedkar.

   Emphasizing the importance of social equality and equity to achieve the real meaning of independence.

10. Chandra Shekhar Azad.

    The Jallianwala Bagh massacre had left a profound mark on him. He used the slogan to convey that he will continue fighting for the country.

DID YOU KNOW?

Lord Mountbatten declared 15 August as the date for India's day of Independence to commemorate and coincide with the surrender of Japan to the Allied forces at the end of the Second World War in 1945.

13

THE PRESS

1. The publication of which journal, founded and edited by Raja Ram Mohan Roy, was the first newspaper to be stopped due to the implementation of the Licensing Regulation of 1823 by John Adams, the then acting Governor General of India? The Act primarily penalized Indian-language newspapers that did not have a licence.
2. Who is known as 'the liberator of the Indian press' for safeguarding the interests of vernacular newspapers in India and relaxing the restrictions from the British government in India?
3. The Vernacular Press Act of 1878 was implemented by Lord Lytton with a view to repressing seditious writing in vernacular dailies and providing preferential treatment to English dailies. Moreover, the publishers were required to provide an undertaking and a security amount to the district magistrate, whose decisions were to be final and binding on any action, without any provision for further appeal. By what other name is the

Act known, which signifies 'the choking of the press'?

4. In a bid to escape the imperialistic and exploitative features of the Vernacular Press Act, which interesting step did Sisir Kumar Ghosh and Moti Lal Ghosh take to safeguard India's first daily, *Amrita Bazar Patrika*?

5. *Navjivan* and *Qaumi Awaz*, respectively, were the Hindi and Urdu versions of which newspaper founded by Pandit Jawaharlal Nehru in 1938 as a tool to win India's Independence?

6. After the murder of Walter Charles Rand, the plague commissioner of Poona, by the Chapekar brothers, Bal Gangadhar Tilak was arrested and tried on charges of sedition against the British for publishing two articles in his newspaper *Kesari*. One of the articles was a report on the justification of the murder of Afzal Khan by Maharaj Shivaji, while the other was a rhetorical poem. Identify the poem.

7. In the backdrop of the riot that broke out between the Parsee and the Muslim communities in Mumbai in 1851, a newspaper was founded by Dadabhai Naoroji and Kharshedji Cama for giving voice to the grievances of the poor and for propagating the Zoroastrian concept of peace and brotherhood. Moreover, during the Revolt of 1857, the newspaper played a pivotal role in voicing the opinions of Indians against the exploitation of the British. Identify this lesser-known newspaper.

8. Which weekly Urdu newspaper founded by the famous freedom activist Maulana Abul Kalam Azad in 1912 was shut down by the British government under the

regressive and restrictive provisions of the Press Act of 1914?

9. Established and founded in 1853 by Girish Chandra Ghosh, this famous Indian newspaper published a play titled *Nil Darpan* and launched a movement against the British, urging Indian farmers to stop cultivating indigo for white traders. Identify the newspaper, which was later taken over by Ishwar Chandra Vidyasagar.

10. This popular Indian newspaper was founded in erstwhile Madras in 1878 by a group of four law students and two teachers, who were known as the Triplicane Six. The newspaper later played a pioneering role in raising the Indian voice against the British Raj in India. Identify the newspaper, the foundation of which was laid by G. Subramania Iyer.

ANSWERS

1. *Mirat-Ul-Akhbar*.
2. Lord Charles Metcalfe.

   He implemented the Press Act of 1835, also known as the Metcalfe Act. It led to the rapid growth of newspapers in India.
3. The Gagging Act.
4. *Amrita Bazar Patrika* was originally a Bengali daily. After the implementation of the Vernacular Press Act, it was turned into an English daily overnight.
5. *National Herald*. The newspaper was relaunched in 2017 in Bengaluru.
6. *Shivaji's Utterances*.

7. *Rast Goftar* (The Truth Teller).
8. *Al-Hilal.*
9. *The Hindu Patriot.*
10. *The Hindu.*

DID YOU KNOW?

Udant Martand (The Rising Sun) is the first Hindi-language newspaper in India, which was established on 30 May 1826 by Pandit Jugal Kishore Shukla in erstwhile Calcutta. Today, Hindi Journalism Day, or Hindi Patrika Diwas, is celebrated on 30 May every year to commemorate the beginning of *Udant Martand.*

14

POLICIES ON EDUCATION

1. During the rule of the East India Company in 1791, the Sanskrit College (now known as Sampurnanand Sanskrit Vishwavidyalaya) was sanctioned in Benares under the then Governor General Lord Cornwallis. Who first proposed the idea of the establishment of the college for the development and preservation of Sanskrit grammar in India?
2. In an attempt to make English civil servants better understand Indian culture, tradition, custom, law and language during the Company rule in India, which historic college was set up in Calcutta by Lord Wellesley on 10 July 1800?
3. Devised and conceptualized by Lord Macaulay, this educational theory was put into action for better administration and governance, where the British planned to educate a small section of upper- and middle-class individuals in English, who would, in turn, pass on the education to the masses in a vernacular language, thus acting as an interpreter between the

government and the masses. It created a class which was 'Indian in blood and colour but English in taste, opinions, morals and intellect'. Identify the theory.

4. Dakshinaranjan Mukherjee was one of the former leaders of the Young Bengal group of the nineteenth century. He once gave a loan of ₹60,000 to an Englishman named David Hare. However, unable to repay the loan, Hare gave a piece of land to Mukherjee instead. Later, in 1849, Mukherjee donated the land to a British lawyer in India for setting up the first secular girls' school in India. Identify the historic school, which was eventually named after the English lawyer.
5. The recommendation of this official report formulated in 1854 laid the basis of the first comprehensive plan for the spread of education in India. The features included setting up of education departments in every province, government schools in every district and universities in big Indian cities. Identify the report, which is also famously known as the 'Magna Carta of English Education in India'.
6. The recommendation of which commission in India led to the division of secondary education in India to literary education that would continue up to university level and vocational education for students interested in a commercial career?
7. Under the provision of which Act did the British government gain paramount powers in matters related to universities and the nomination of fellowships? It was the same Act that Gopal Krishna Gokhale called a 'retrograde measure', as it tried to strengthen

imperialism and destroy nationalist feelings. Which Act was this?

8. This educational scheme was formulated in 1937 under the chairmanship of Zakir Husain and based on Mahatma Gandhi's ideas on education in a series of articles in his weekly, *Harijan*, which had the basic principle of 'learning with activity'. It is noteworthy that the inclusion of study and the practice of a basic handicraft in the syllabus was first propounded in this scheme. Identify the scheme.
9. Which historic private Bill, later rejected, was moved in the Imperial Legislative Council on 19 March 1910, which is regarded as the first Bill in India to suggest the idea of free and compulsory education for boys between the ages of 6 and 10?
10. Which famous political leader is credited with successfully moving a Bill in the Bombay Legislative Council for the introduction of compulsory primary education in the Bombay municipality, known as the Municipality Primary Education Act, 1918? This is historically thought to prelude the foundation of the Right to Education in Independent India.

ANSWERS

1. Jonathan Duncan.
2. Fort William College.
3. The Downward Filtration Theory.
4. Bethune School. Named after John Elliot Drinkwater Bethune, the English barrister.

5. Wood's Despatch. Named after the British member of parliament Sir Charles Wood.
6. Hunter Commission, 1882. Named after W.W. Hunter.
7. The Indian Universities Act, 1904.
8. The Wardha Scheme of Basic Education.
9. Gokhale Bill.
10. Vithalbhai Patel. The Act is also known as the 'Patel Act'.

DID YOU KNOW?

The Serampore College in West Bengal is the oldest functional college in India. Three English missionaries, William Carey, Joshua Marshman and William Ward, established it in 1818.

15

REVOLUTIONARY HISTORY–II

1. A distinguished Independence activist, he was fondly described as 'Sher-e-Ballia' (Tiger of Ballia) by Jawaharlal Nehru and Subhas Chandra Bose for leading the Quit India Movement in Ballia, Uttar Pradesh. Identify the personality, who formed a parallel government in Ballia and released all arrested Congress leaders of the locality.
2. This famous Indian freedom fighter and politician was a founding member of the Naujawan Bharat Sabha, which rallied thousands of students and youths to participate in the nationalist cause of freedom. He was also the founding member of the Jamia Millia Islamia university, which came into existence in 1920. Later, in 1921, he established Swaraj Ashrams in Amritsar, where he trained young men for national work and to promote Hindu-Muslim unity. Identify the great personality, who is best remembered for his vicious protests against the Rowlatt Acts of 1919.
3. He was an illiterate cotton-mill worker from Bombay,

who vehemently supported the cause of development of labour unions. In the backdrop of Gandhi's Swadeshi Movement, he resonated with the vision of Swadeshi and made it his life's goal to defeat the forces of economic colonialism using non-violent means. On 12 December 1930, he lay down in front of a moving truck carrying foreign-made clothes in the Kalbadevi area of Bombay to prevent its entry through the area. He was mercilessly run over by the truck. Identify this freedom fighter and revolutionary who gave his life at the young age of 22.

4. Identify the Indian poet and freedom activist from Himachal Pradesh who spread Gandhian messages through his fiery patriotic poems and songs. The news of the death sentence handed to Bhagat Singh, Rajguru and Sukhdev in 1931 had so deeply impacted him that he vowed to wear black clothes until India achieved Independence. Thus he was also affectionately known as the 'Siyahposh Jarnail' (the Black General). Later, in 1937, Pandit Jawaharlal Nehru conferred upon him the title of 'Pahari Gandhi' for his stellar contribution towards Independence in Himachal. Who am I talking about?

5. The Punjabi book *Gadar Di Dhee* ______ ______, written by S. Kesar Singh, is an account of which famous female freedom fighter of the Ghadar Party, who distributed arms to members while posing as a journalist?

6. The English poet Sir Henry Newbolt's poem *Gillespie* is a vivid account of the historic incident in India that took place on 10 July 1806, which is considered the

precursor of the Revolt of 1857. Identify the landmark incident.

7. Considered the first in the long series of tribal resistance against the British in India, this tribal rebellion broke out in 1772. The revolt was against the exploitation of tribal resources in the wake of the 1770 famine in Santhal Pargana, in present-day Jharkhand. Identify the leader who united the Adivasis to defy Lord Clive's policy of 'Divide and Rule'. Also identify the armed rebellion.

8. A lesser-known historical fact is about the leader of the Garhwal Rifles Regiment, who refused and revolted against the British commander who ordered soldiers to fire on thousands of unarmed peaceful Pathan protesters in Peshawar on 23 April 1930, thus preventing another Jallianwala Bagh massacre. Name the Indian soldier, who came to be known as 'the hero of the Peshawar revolt'.

9. Born in Bhopal, he championed the cause of India's freedom from around the world. While in England, he came in close contact with Lala Har Dayal and Raja Mahendra Pratap. Later, in 1915, he became the first prime minister of the Provincial Government of India, established in Kabul, Afghanistan. Identify the Indian revolutionary, in whose memory the present-day Bhopal University has been named.

10. Barrister Attavar Yellappa was one of the greatest patriots from Mangalore (now Mangaluru), who joined the Indian National Army to fight against the British alongside Netaji Subhas Chandra Bose. He

was severely injured while fighting the British in the jungles of Myanmar in the middle of the Second World War and his body could not be found. During the early years, he was instrumental in setting up an institution to manage the funds donated from across the world to the Provincial Indian Government in Rangoon (now Yangon) led by Bose. Identify the institution.

11. On 28 January 1894, hundreds of peasants in the Darrang district of Assam took out a peaceful procession to protest against the British government's policy of imposing exorbitant taxes. However, the officiating commander of the military police, J.R. Berington, ordered soldiers to open fire on the unarmed protesters. The firing led to the death of 140 peasants and several others were severely injured. Also known as 'Assam's Jallianwala Bagh', how is this incident better known in the pages of history?

12. Revolutionaries Pandurang Khankhoje and Pandit Kanshi Ram of the Ghadar Party are credited with forming which organization in Portland, Oregon, in 1908 to organize those individuals living outside India who sought the removal of British colonial rule from India?

13. This great patriot was the prince of Manipur, who became the commander of the Manipur army after the death of his father, Maharaja Chandrakirti Singh, in 1886. He led the rebellion against the British army, which eventually led to the Anglo-Manipur War of 1891. This Manipuri braveheart is also referred to as the 'Lion of Manipur' for his valiant and undaunted efforts to fight the British. He was later hanged

publicly on 13 August 1891. The day is now celebrated as 'Patriot's Day' in Manipur. Identify him.

14. Known as 'Andhra Kesari', he was the first chief minister of the Madras Presidency and later became the chief minister of Andhra Pradesh, created after the partition of the Madras state. He began his career as a lawyer but gave up the practice in 1921 to participate in the Indian freedom movement. He rose to fame in 1928 during the protest against the Simon Commission in Madras. When the British police issued orders to shoot the protesters, he tore open his shirt and dared the police to shoot him. Identify the famous Indian politician and freedom fighter.

15. An eminent nationalist and a literary figure from Assam, he took active part in the Indian freedom movement. During the British rule in Assam, he wrote several Assamese patriotic songs and articles to arouse nationalism among the masses. During the launch of the Swadeshi Movement by Mahatma Gandhi, he founded the Asom Sangrakshini Sabha (Assam Preservation Council) and Asom Jatiyo Mohaxoba (Assam National Congress) to mobilize the people for the cause of Swadeshi. Due to his remarkable contribution during the freedom movement and in the field of Assamese literature, he was given the title of 'Assam Kesari'. Identify the famous personality.

16. He is famously described as the 'Indian Robin Hood', a skilful guerrilla bandit who was active in British India between 1878 and 1889 in Madhya Pradesh. He looted the government treasuries and English people, and distributed the riches to the poor and the needy.

Identify the heroic figure who was affectionately called 'Mama' by the masses.

17. During the launch of the Quit India Movement in 1942, the British government responded by arresting all the major leaders and members of the Congress Working Committee. During this uncertain time, which Indian Independence activist took charge of the remaining session of the Congress?

18. The ceremony of forming India's first Independent government was done with Justice Hiralal Kania as the first chief justice of India, who administered the oath to the new Governor General, who then administered the oath to the first prime minister, Jawaharlal Nehru, and his Cabinet. During the ceremony, only one minister failed to swear in as he was still in hospital after a recent plane crash. Identify this prominent independence activist, who was also the first labour minister of the first interim government in India.

19. Born in Nagwa village in Uttar Pradesh, Mangal Pandey is considered to be the first freedom fighter of modern Indian history, who ignited the spark of freedom that led to the Revolt of 1857 against the British. As a sepoy, he revolted against the use of greased cartridges for the new Enfield rifles. The cartridges were rumoured to be smeared with pig and cow fat, thus creating widespread discontent among the Hindu and Muslim soldiers, leading to the revolt. To which regiment did Mangal Pandey belong?

20. Which left-wing nationalist political party was formed by Subhas Chandra Bose in 1939 as a faction

within the Congress due to rising ideological and perceptional differences between him and Mahatma Gandhi, eventually resulting in his resignation from the presidency of the Indian National Congress?

ANSWERS

1. Chittu Pandey.
2. Saifuddin Kitchlew.
3. Babu Genu Said.
4. Baba Kanshi Ram.
5. Gulab Kaur.
6. The Vellore Mutiny. It was the first instance of a large-scale violent mutiny by Indian sepoys against the East India Company.
7. Tilka Manjhi. Manjhi Rebellion.
8. Chandra Singh Garhwali.
9. Abdul Hafiz Mohamed Barakatullah.
10. Azad Hind Bank.
11. Patharughator Rann (Battle of Patharughat).
12. Indian Independence League.
13. Bir Tikendrajit Singh.
14. Tanguturi Prakasam.
15. Ambikagiri Raichoudhury.
16. Tantia Bhīl.
17. Aruna Asaf Ali.
18. Babu Jagjivan Ram.
19. 34th Bengal Native Infantry.
20. All India Forward Bloc.

DID YOU KNOW?

The present-day Indian Railways owes its existence to the British. It was under Governor General Lord Dalhousie that the first train ran in India from Bombay to Thane on 16 April 1853. It is noteworthy that the primary reason for the introduction of the railways in India was quick transportation of minerals and non-mineral items to mainland India for the interests and profits of the British.

16

TAKE IT EASY

1. The resolutions on Fundamental Rights and National Economic Policy were passed in which of the following sessions of the Indian National Congress?
   a. Belgaum, 1934
   b. Lahore, 1929
   c. Karachi, 1931
   d. Faizpur, 1936
2. Which among the following viceroys was associated with the Ilbert Bill Controversy?
   a. Lord Curzon
   b. Lord Lytton
   c. Lord Ripon
   d. Lord Hardinge
3. Subhas Chandra Bose was re-elected the president of the Indian National Congress at the Tripuri Session in 1939 by defeating Gandhiji's candidate. Who was the candidate?
   a. Dr Rajendra Prasad
   b. J.B. Kriplani
   c. Pattabhi Sitaramayya
   d. Nellie Sengupta

4. The 'Mappila rebellion' is associated with which of the following states?
   a. Bihar
   b. Gujarat
   c. Punjab
   d. Kerala
5. With which of the following policies of the British is the comment 'no dalil, no vakil, no appeal' associated?
   a. The Communal Award, 1932
   b. The Simon Commission, 1928
   c. The Rowlatt Acts, 1919
   d. The Vernacular Press Act, 1878
6. The Hunter Commission was appointed by the British to probe matters related to:
   a. The Chauri Chaura incident
   b. The Jallianwala Bagh tragedy
   c. The Khilafat Movement
   d. The Non-Cooperation Movement
7. Who planted the 'Tree of Liberty' at Srirangapatna?
   a. Hyder Ali
   b. Tipu Sultan
   c. Chin Quilich Khan
   d. Murshid Quli Khan
8. Which of the following personalities started the newspapers *New India* and *Commonweal*?
   a. Madan Mohan Malviya
   b. S. Subramaniyam Iyer
   c. Annie Besant
   d. Lala Lajpat Rai
9. The only session of the Indian National Congress that

was presided over by Mahatma Gandhi was held at:

a. Belgaum
b. Faizpur
c. Allahabad
d. Karachi

10. What was the name of the first newspaper to announce the Partition of Bengal on 6 July 1905?

a. *Swaraj*
b. *Sanjivani*
c. *Kalantar*
d. *Anandabazar Patrika*

11. During the British era in India, several Indian activists and students studying in foreign countries formed the Indian Independence Committee. This was set up in which country?

a. France
b. The United Kingdom
c. Germany
d. The United States of America

12. Who among the following founded the 'Depressed Classes Mission Society of India' to provide education and social rights to the depressed class?

a. Dr B.R. Ambedkar
b. Vitthal Ramji Shinde
c. Annabhau Sathe
d. Shantabai Kamble

13. Which of the following was the first satyagraha movement inspired by Mahatma Gandhi during the Indian freedom movement?

a. Bardoli Satyagraha

b. Kheda Satyagraha
c. Champaran Satyagraha
d. Ahmedabad Satyagraha

14. At which of the following places did Jayaprakash Narayan convene the first All India Congress Socialists' Conference in 1934?
    a. Lucknow
    b. Patna
    c. Gaya
    d. Kolkata

15. There were three people in the Indian National Congress whose influence and persuasion led to a sort of agreement between the Congress and the British, leading to talks between Gandhi and Lord Irwin, commonly known as the Gandhi-Irwin Pact. Who among the following was not among these three?
    a. Tej Bahadur Sapru
    b. M.R. Jayakar
    c. V.S. Srinivasa Shastri
    d. Purushottam Das Tandon

16. About which of the following books did Mahatma Gandhi say, 'It brought about an instantaneous and practical transformation in my life'?
    a. *Anna Karenina*
    b. *War and Peace*
    c. *The Odyssey*
    d. *Unto This Last*

17. Who among the following was the president of the Indian National Congress at the time of Independence?
    a. Dr Rajendra Prasad

b. J.B. Kriplani
c. Dr Bhimrao Ambedkar
d. Jawaharlal Nehru

18. The first explanation for the difference of opinion on extremism in the Indian National Congress was written down by which of the following personalities in a series of articles titled 'New Lamps for Old' in a Bombay newspaper?
a. Bal Gangadhar Tilak
b. Aurobindo Ghose
c. Bipin Chandra Pal
d. Mahatma Gandhi

19. Which of the following female freedom activists can be related with the Chittagong armory raid, along with Surya Sen?
a. Kalpana Datta
b. Bhikaji Cama
c. Basanti Devi
d. Sucheta Kriplani

20. The Vernacular Press Act was repealed by which of the following viceroys of India?
a. Lord Lansdowne
b. Lord Ripon
c. Lord Dufferin
d. Lord Lytton

ANSWERS

1. c. Karachi, 1931.
2. c. Lord Ripon.

3. c. Pattabhi Sitaramayya.
4. d. Kerala.
5. c. The Rowlatt Acts, 1919.
6. b. The Jallianwala Bagh tragedy.
7. b. Tipu Sultan.
8. c. Annie Besant.
9. a. Belgaum.
10. b. *Sanjivani.*
11. c. Germany. It was also known as the 'Berlin Committee'.
12. b. Vitthal Ramji Shinde.
13. c. Champaran Satyagraha.
14. b. Patna.
15. d. Purushottam Das Tandon.
16. d. *Unto This Last*, written by John Ruskin.
17. b. J.B. Kriplani.
18. b. Aurobindo Ghose.
19. a. Kalpana Datta.
20. b. Lord Ripon

DID YOU KNOW?

During his stay in South Africa in the early 1900s, Mahatma Gandhi founded three football clubs, all named Passive Resisters Soccer Club. He used sports to propagate non-violence and unity.

AUTHOR'S NOTE

I hope the readers liked the book. I have tried my best to strike a balance between curiosity and creativity, fundas and fundamentals.

No stone was left unturned in my attempt to dig deep into the annals of our glorious past while framing each question.

Framing quiz questions is an arduous task.

Nothing would give me greater satisfaction than if the readers had an enlightening, enriching and fulfilling experience.

ACKNOWLEDGEMENTS

I extend my sincere gratitude to the quizzing community across India for keeping my curiosity alive.

It was possible for the idea of this book to materialize because Rupa Publications reached out to me and encouraged me to write it. I enjoyed the whole experience. Thanks to the Rupa team for this wonderful opportunity.

I am thankful to Barnali Hazarika for constantly encouraging me to complete this work on time. I would not have been able to if it were not for her continuous bickering.

I also take this opportunity to thank my dear friend Subhasish Sarma Thakur for being a mentor throughout the writing of this book.

I am thankful to my teachers and my alma maters for giving me an environment that gave birth to, nurtured and sustained my quizzing journey.